MICHELLE ROBINSON
TEN FAT SAUSAGES
ILLUSTRATIONS: TOR FREEMAN
ANDERSEN PRESS

Ten fat sausages, sizzling in a pan.
One went POP and the other went...

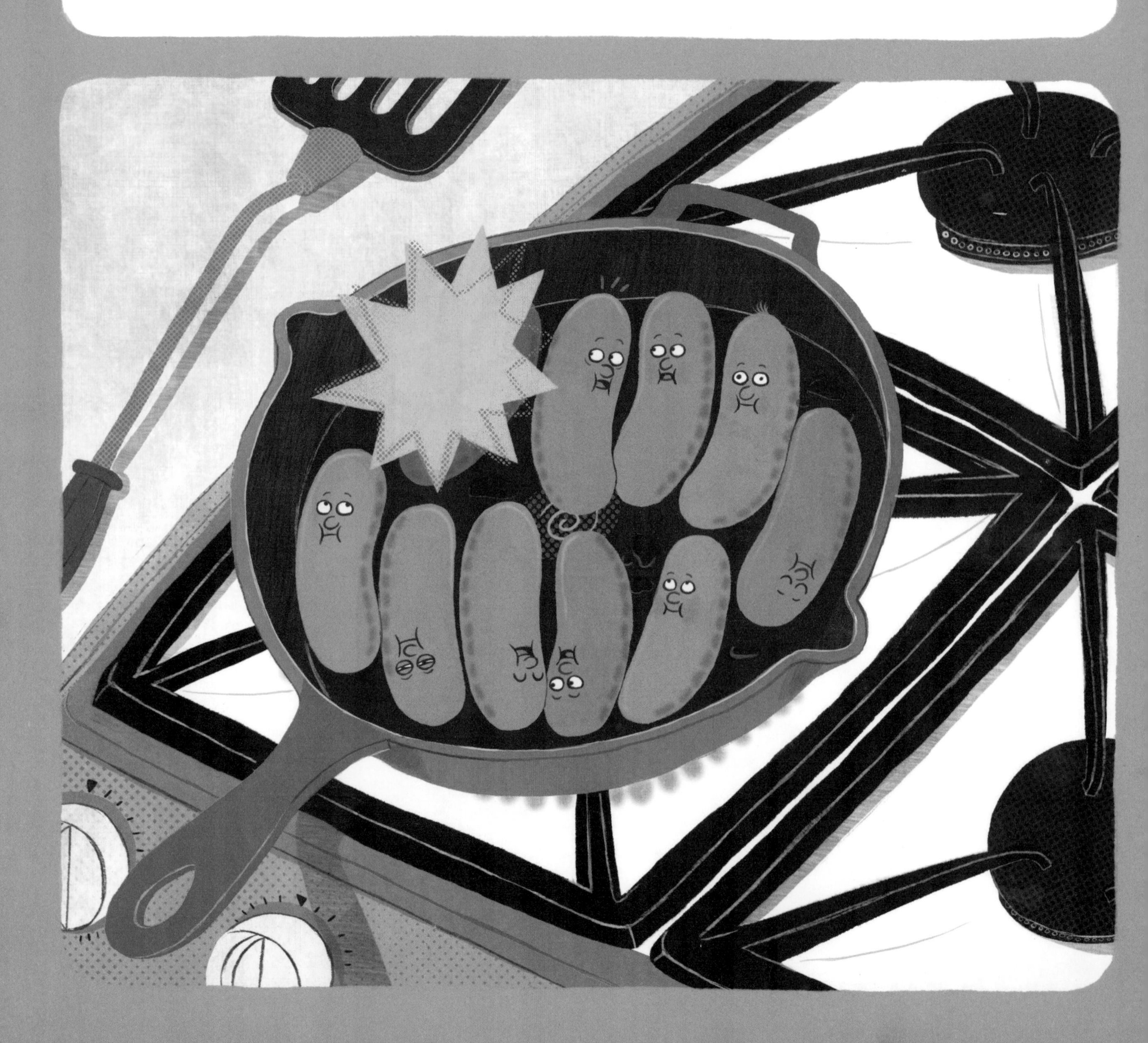

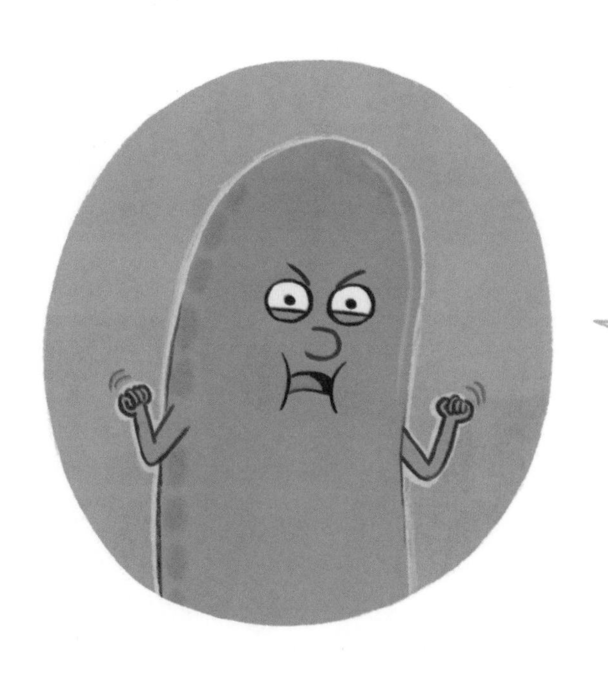

Hang on a minute!
I do not like this.
The fridge went hummm,
but the pan goes hissss.
Well, I won't go BANG
and I won't go POP.

And Sausage Number Two went hop, hop, hop.

He was doing quite well till
they pulled out the plug.

BEAR SHINE
A WHIRLPOOL!
He spluttered and reached for the chain.
But Sausage Number Two
WHOOSHED straight down the drain.

Eight fat sausages, sizzling in a pan.
One went POP and the other went...

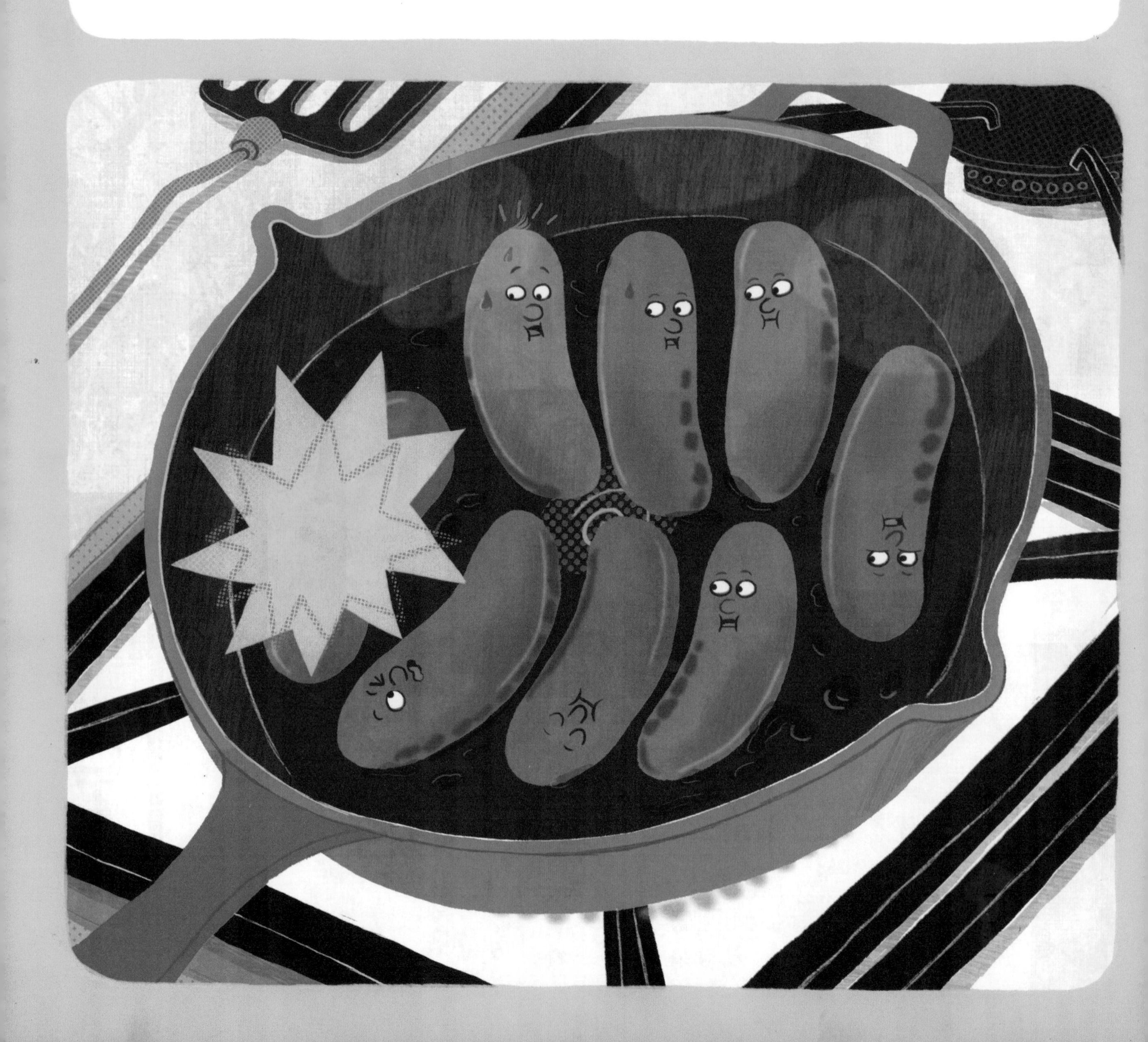

HANG on a minute!
I've had quite enough
of sitting around in
this hot, oily stuff.
Well, I won't go BANG
and I won't go POP.

And Sausage Number Four went hop, hop, hop.

Over the counter
and into a bowl.
"This is more comfortable."

"Yes, on the whole
I am far better off.
But this switch is a mystery..."

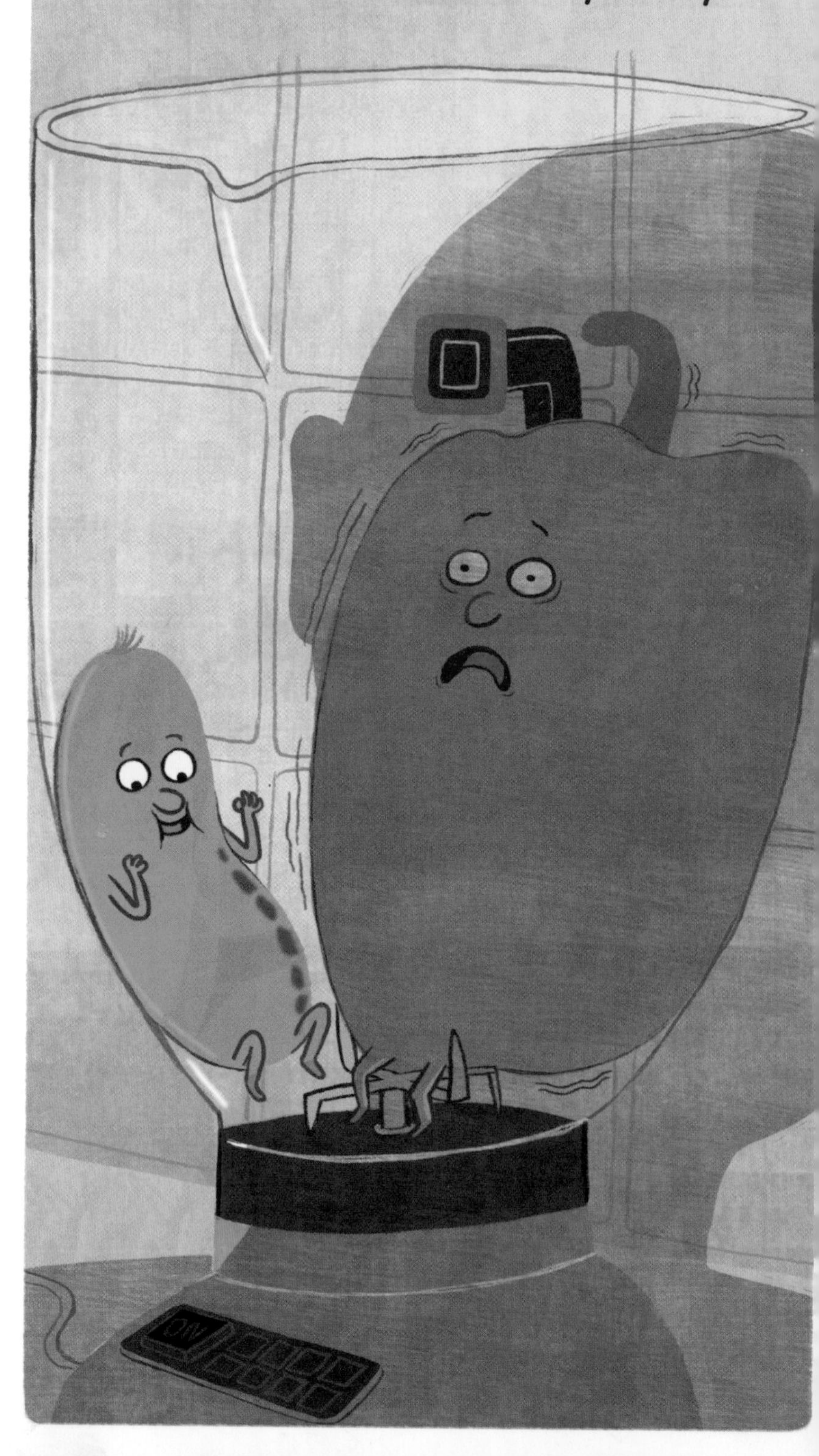

ON went the switch:
Sausage Four was history.
YUM

Six fat sausages, sizzling in a pan.
One went POP and the other went...

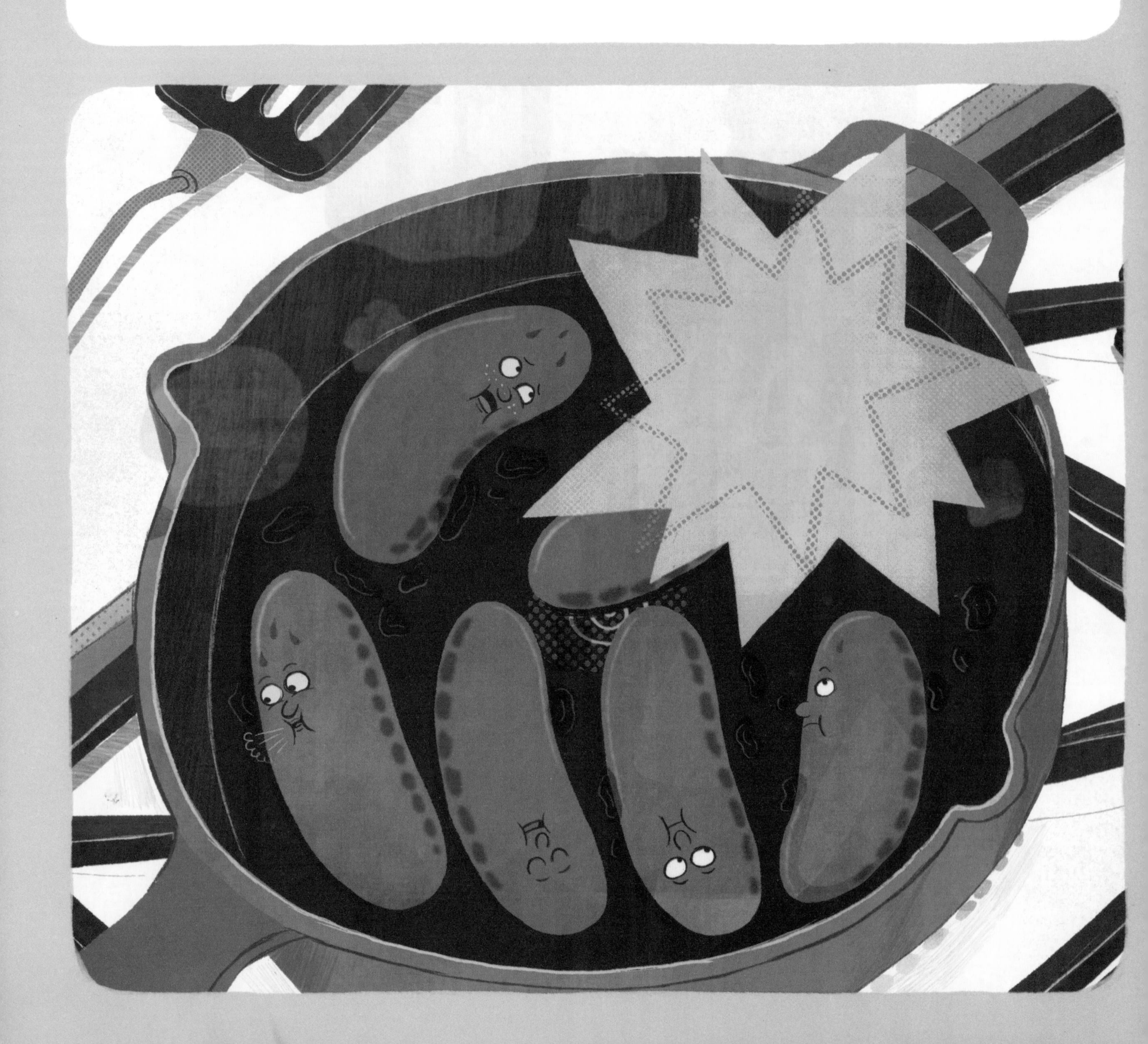

HANG on a minute.
I want to break free!
I don't want to end up
as somebody's tea.
Well, I won't go BANG
and I won't go POP.

And Sausage Number Six went hop, hop, hop.

Straight up the cookbooks
and onto the fridge.

Over the wide open Freezer Top Ridge.

"The whole world awaits.
I'm a freewheeling man.
GIDDY UP!"
Sausage Six was
flung by the fan.

Four fat sausages, sizzling in a pan.
One went POP and the other went...

HANG on a minute,
that was my best friend.
She didn't deserve
such a terrible end.
Well, I won't go bang
and I won't go pop.

And Sausage Number Eight went hop, hop, hop.

Down from the counter
and over the floor.

Past the cat's bed.
"If I just reach the door..."

"Freedom awaits - I can make it!
Oh, drat."
A little less sausage
and a LOT more cat.

Two fat sausages, sizzling in a pan.
"Try not to POP. We'll escape – I've a plan."

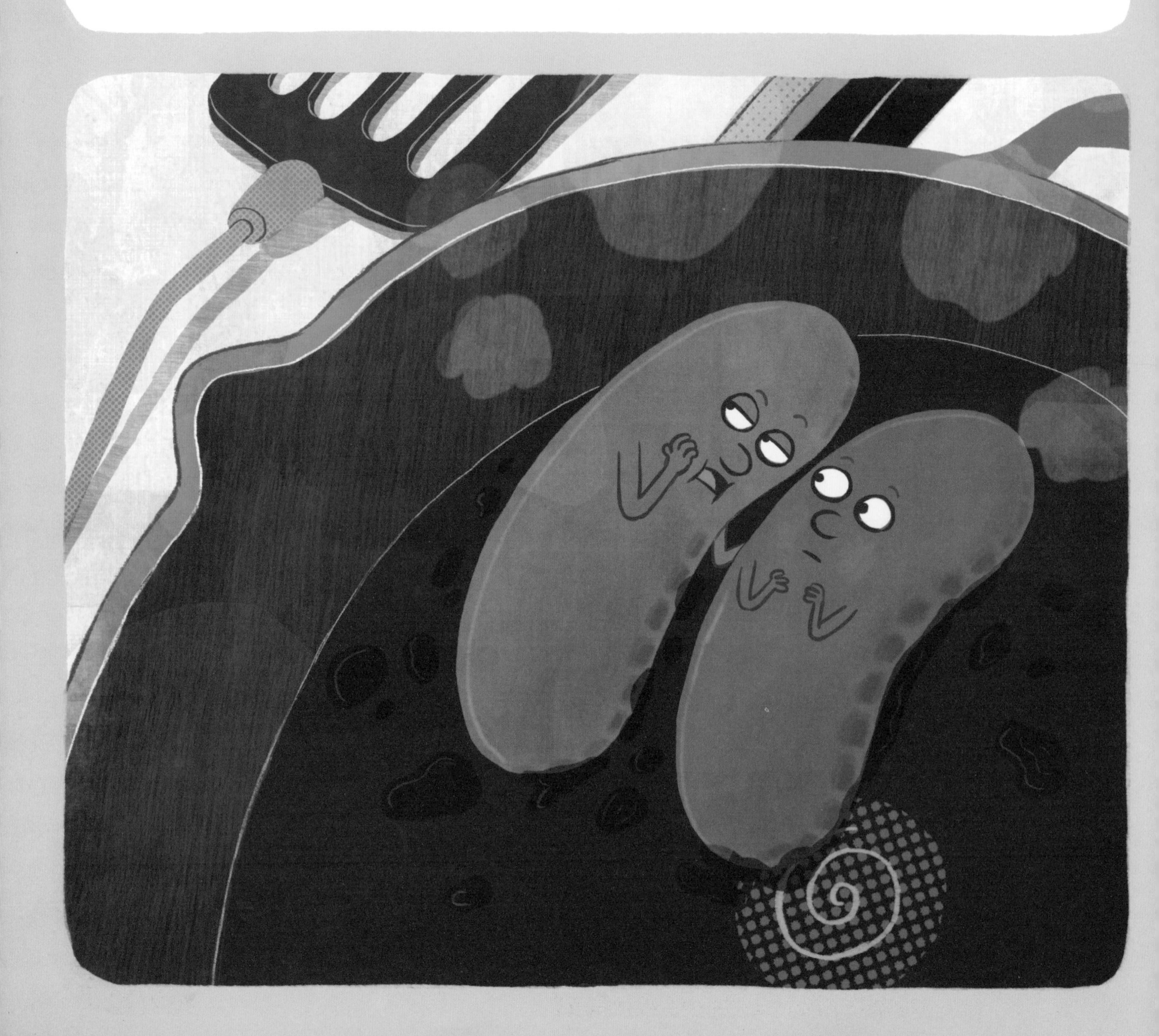

BANG!

yelled the sausage,
and

POP!

said his brother.

The hob was switched off.
They embraced one another.
Now, as sausages go,
that last plan was quite clever.
Might this pair survive?

Over the counter they went at a run.
"Let's hide in this squishy thing. Whee! This is fun!"
They hulaed in onion rings, danced in red sauce.
Two silly sausages...

One main course.

stard

BEAR
SHINE

BEAR SHINE
101 WAYS WITH SAUSAGES
A.P. WIENER
101 WAYS WITH SAUSAGES